The Big Tale of Little Peppa

Once upon a time, Peppa's best friend,
Suzy Sheep, came to play.

"I've got something to show you,"
said Suzy.

"Look!"

"It's me," said Suzy.

"You're not a baby, Suzy," said Peppa, shaking her head.

"This is an old photo," Suzy explained. "It was taken when I was little."

Peppa snorted. Suzy was being **very silly** today!

Suzy pointed at Peppa. "In the olden days you were a baby too!" she said.

"No, I wasn't!"
said Peppa.

"Yes, you were,"
insisted Suzy.
"Ask your mummy."

Peppa and Suzy raced inside. Mummy Pig was working on the computer.

"Mummy!" cried Peppa. "Suzy is making up stories!"

"No, I'm not," Suzy said crossly. Peppa told Mummy Pig about Suzy's silly idea that they used to be babies.

"But you **were** a baby, Peppa!" said Mummy Pig.

Mummy Pig took a look on the computer.
"Who do you think this is, Peppa?" Mummy Pig asked.
Peppa thought that the baby looked a bit like her cousin.
"Is it Baby Alexander?" she asked.

"No!" replied Mummy Pig.
"That's **you** as a baby, Peppa."

Hee! Hee!

Hee! Hee!

Suzy and Peppa giggled.
They'd never seen Baby Peppa before!

George and Daddy Pig came in to see what all the fuss was about.

"Look, Daddy!" said Peppa. "That's me as a baby!"

"I remember it," said Daddy Pig. "That photo was taken on our first day in this house."

"What do you mean?" asked Peppa.

Daddy Pig told Peppa, Suzy and George that they had moved into their house when Peppa was very little.

"We brought all our things on the top of our car," he said.

"Mummy Pig put some pictures up," said Daddy Pig.

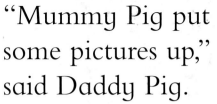

"Daddy Pig put up a shelf . . ." said Mummy Pig.

". . . and Grandpa Pig made us a lovely flower garden!" she continued.

Peppa and Suzy went outside to see what
Grandpa Pig's lovely flower garden
looked like now.

It had completely
disappeared!

"Daddy Pig looked after the flower garden," sighed Mummy Pig.

"Er . . ." said Daddy Pig,
"we had the wrong kind
of soil for flowers."

"Was Suzy my friend in the olden days?" asked Peppa.
Daddy Pig nodded. "Of course!" he said.

Hee! Hee!

"You and Suzy have always been **best friends**."

Peppa wondered what games she played with Suzy when they were little.

"Did we **jump** up and down in muddy puddles?"

"No, Peppa," laughed Mummy Pig. "You were babies. You couldn't even walk!"

"What did we do when we were babies, Mrs Pig?" asked Suzy.

"You cried . . .

you burped . . .

and you laughed!"

Suzy and Peppa burst out laughing.

Hee! Hee!

Hee! Hee!

"Baby Peppa!"

"Baby Suzy!"

"Then you grew into toddlers," continued Mummy Pig.
"But where was George?" Peppa asked.

"He was a baby in my
tummy!"
said Mummy Pig.

Daddy Pig went to find the camera.
"Let's take a photo of you now," he suggested.

Peppa, Suzy and George did their **best smiles.**

Click!

Little or big, Peppa will always love jumping up and down in

muddy
puddles!